For Juliana, Maggie and all grannies everywhere — A.E.

For Bob, Jocelyn and family, with love — B.C.

BLOOMSBURY CHILDREN'S BOOKS
Bloomsbury Publishing Plc
50 Bedford Square, London, WC1B 3DP, UK

BLOOMSBURY, BLOOMSBURY CHILDREN'S BOOKS and the Diana logo are trademarks of Bloomsbury Publishing Plc

First published in Great Britain 2021 by Bloomsbury Publishing Plc

A catalogue record for this book is available from the British Library

ISBN: 978 1 4088 8839 1 (HB)
ISBN: 978 1 4088 8841 4 (PB)
ISBN: 978 1 4088 8840 7 (eBook)

1 3 5 7 9 10 8 6 4 2

Printed and bound in China by Leo Paper Products, Heshan, Guangdong

All papers used by Bloomsbury Publishing Plc are natural, recyclable products from wood grown in well managed forests.
The manufacturing processes conform to the environmental regulations of the country of origin.

To find out more about our authors and books visit www.bloomsbury.com and sign up for our newsletters

STOP THAT DINOSAUR!

written by
Alex English

illustrated by
Ben Cort

BLOOMSBURY
CHILDREN'S BOOKS
LONDON OXFORD NEW YORK NEW DELHI SYDNEY

I was in my Granny's kitchen eating extra-special cake,
when the walls began to tremble
and the roof began to SHAKE.
The windowpanes all rattled
and there was a MIGHTY

ROA

R !

KNOCK!

KNOCK!

KNOCK!

Ring! Ring! Ring!

WHO was at the door?

Granny opened up the door,
I heard her SCREAM and then . . .

. . . a **brontosaurus** snatched her up
and ran away again!

That dinosaur was very fast and nimble on its feet.

So I jumped right on my scooter . . .

and I **WHIZZED** off down the street.

I chased it to the playground,
towards the pond,
and past the slide.

But it showed no sign of **STOPPING**,
however hard I tried.

A duck was on my handlebars,
I couldn't see the floor.
But I kept on scooting,
shouting out . . .

I chased it up the high street,

past the shops and the town hall.

But it showed no sign of STOPPING – no it didn't slow at all!

I started scooting faster than I **EVER** had before.

And I kept on chasing,

shouting out . . .

I chased it through the long grass, past a farm and through the fields.
But did that dino **STOP**?
Oh, no — however fast my wheels.

My shoes were wet and muddy
and my legs were getting sore.
But I kept on scooting,
shouting out . . .

"STOP that DINOSAUR!"

I chased it down the hillside,
then I lost it in the wood.

I couldn't see it anywhere – was Granny gone for good?

My eyes filled up with tears and my knees began to knock.
What would I tell my mummy when she came at six o'clock?

I scooted even faster,
I just had to get Gran back!
But my shoelace caught a tree root
and I skidded off the track.

I flew right through the air
and then I wobbled to the side.

I scraped my knee
and bumped my bum.

And then I heard a sniffle
and a rustle in the leaves.
That dinosaur came creeping out
from in-between the trees.

"Where's my Gran?" I whimpered.
"I need her back, you see,
I really, really miss her —
she's the only Gran for me."

"I'm sorry," said the dinosaur.
"It's wrong to steal from you.
But your Granny looked so friendly
that I longed to have one too.

I've heard grans read you stories

and they make you apple pie.

They kiss your bruises better
and they hug you when you cry.

I never would have done it
    if I'd had one of my own –
    but we dinos don't have grannies,
    we dinos are ALONE."

"Here she is," the dino said.

"I'll bother you no more."

But . . .

"NOT SO FAST!"
we shouted.

"STOP please, DINOSAUR!"

"There's no need to be lonely –
would you like to come for tea?
There's extra-special cake at home,
and plenty there for three."

So we went back to my Granny's
where the dino-chase began . . .

Now Dino drops in every week
so we can **share** my Gran!